This book belongs to:

···

Be kind to one another, tender hearted, forgiving one another (a) – The Bible

For AJ & Annabelle

You inspire me to do better and be better every day.

Thank you to my Mum & John Hagley for helping me prepare this book.

Thank you to my family and friends for supporting me always.

You will never know how grateful I am to God for you.

Author: Anusjka R.E.

Email: hello@sidthekindestkid.com

Website: www.sidthekindestkid.com

Please direct all enquiries to the author.

ISBN: 978-1-83853-985-6

Sid the Kindest Kid

Ben Learns to Be Kind

Anusjka R.E.

UK   NIGERIA   TRINIDAD & TOBAGO   USA   AUSTRALIA   INDIA

Ben **snatched** the train Kameron and Suzy were playing with.

He said, "Suzy was stupid," and he ran away.

Ben was taller and bigger than the other children in his class. The children were scared of him because, **he was mean** to them all the time.

The only time he spoke to them was to call them horrible names. He would also bump into them on purpose and take their toys.

He never **smiled**, and he never said **please** or **thank you.**

The children were happy to be back to school after a long summer holiday. After lunch on the first day of the new term, most of the children went out to play on the playground. But Sid, Kameron, and Suzy stayed indoors to play with the train set.

They all missed **playing** with the school's toy train set.

Kameron really **loved trains.** He knew all about overground and underground trains.

Kameron told his friends he loved going to visit his cousins on the holiday breaks, because his mum always took him on the underground train.

"The underground trains were quite noisy and had lots of people going everywhere," Kameron said.

Sid asked, "Don't all those people and all that noise make you scared?"

"No," Kameron said, "my mum holds my hand really tight. I like seeing all the different faces."

That's when Kameron said that the **first** underground railway in the whole **world** was in **London.**

"Wow!" Suzy said. "I have never been on the underground train. It sounds like lots of **fun.**"

Just then, Ben ran into the classroom, **kicked** the train tracks, which Kameron, Sid, and Suzy had just completed building, and **ran off.**

Sid picked up one of the trains and ran after
Ben the bully.

What do you think Sid did next?

Sid caught up to Ben and asked,

"Would you like to play with me?"

Ben was very surprised. Ben said, "Why did you ask? No one likes to play with me! No one likes me."

Sid said, "If you want anyone to play with you, you have to **be kind.** You are always being mean to everyone."

I am sure they will be happy to play with you if you said, **"Hello, please,** and **thank you."** You can even ask them to play with you...with a **smile.** They just might say yes!"

Sid and Ben sat down and played with the train together.

The other children found them sitting on the floor in the corridor. Ben said, "Sorry for being mean."

Then he asked with a smile, "Do you want to join in?" Ben was surprised that they said yes! He felt really happy inside. Kameron told Ben all he knew about the overground and underground trains.

Ben learned to be kind and decided that he would not be mean.

He made **new friends** and enjoyed playing with them.

Ben said, "Chugga, Chugga, Chugga," and Kameron said, "SCREECH!" They all started laughing.

"This is so much fun," Sid said!

I hope you loved reading *Ben Learns to Be Kind* together!

This is the 2nd book in the Sid the Kindest Kid book series. Go ahead and get the 1st book in the series, Sweets, Sweets, Sweets which is all about sharing.

Discussion:

1. Why do you think Ben was being mean?
2. Why did the other children get along with each other?
3. What advice did Sid give to Ben, to help him make friends?

Visit **sidthekindestkid.com** for more about kindness and free resources.

#sidthekindestkid

- Anusjka R.E.

Printed in Poland
by Amazon Fulfillment
Poland Sp. z o.o., Wrocław

64373286R00021